Five Worlds Apart

Four Short Stories

K. Harper

*To Grace,
Happy reading
from the author Kai*

Copyright © 2023 K.Harper

All rights reserved.

ISBN: 979-8-3959-4595-2

Four Short Stories

Maya, Amy, Chris & Javier

Written by K.Harper

DEDICATION

This book is dedicated to my very patient and extremely supportive family.

CONTENTS

1. Taking Control – Maya's Story   Pg 9
2. Run Chris Run – Chris' Shoes   Pg 26
3. No one likes Being Lonely - Javier   Pg 45
4. Hide and Seek – Amy's World   Pg 63

TAKING CONTROL – MAYA'S STORY

"We're nearly there Maya," said Verity, as the car pulled away from the traffic lights.

Maya opened her eyes slowly and looked out of the passenger side window.

"How long was I asleep for?" yawned Maya.

"Oh not too long dear," replied Verity. "There it is."

Maya followed her mother's finger, which pointed to what she could make out to be the top of the Capel Manor Boarding School building; it was just as it was in the school brochure. She was able to make out the ornate and perfectly rounded clock that sat nestled between the two pillars which ran down to the main entrance.

> "Wow," whispered Maya as she marvelled at how much bigger the building felt, now that she was able to see it up close.

'Turn left in 50 yards and your destination will be on the right.'

Maya's thoughts were disrupted abruptly by the Sat Nav. Her mother pulled into the nearest parking space and switched off the engine. She then turned her body to face Maya.

> "Are you sure that you're okay hun?" she asked, whilst she stroked Maya's hair.

She looked up at her mother and nodded.

Maya strongly resembled her mother, they

were both petite, of mixed ethnicity and both had an abundance of long, curly brown hair. Though Verity's hair was slightly darker in colour than Maya's. They had travelled from West Hampstead that morning and had luckily avoided the usual bouts of traffic that they would encounter when driving to Kent.

> "I want you to know how proud I am of you Maya and how brave I think you are."

Maya smiled.

> "Not many twelve-year-olds would be able to keep it all together; knowing that they were going off to a school far away from their parents."

Maya reached out and wiped a tear from her mother's face.

> "Don't cry mum, it's not that bad, besides, Uncle Andrew will take care of me remember?"

> "I know, I know," said Verity, whilst she tried her best to keep more tears from forming.

"It's just, I'm going to miss you that's all."

"I'm going to miss you too mum," replied Maya as she reached over to comfort her.

"Just promise me you won't pull any pranks on anyone Maya. Remember what happened last time?"

Maya remembered all too well what had happened the last few times she had let her emotions rule her; and cast her mind back to when she was just six years old.

Having always been quite small for her age, she had always struggled to join in with some of the games that the other girls played and consequently found it hard to make friends. Maya found it particularly difficult to join in with the games that were led by Harriet Armstrong. Harriet was tall for her age and broad-shouldered. She had short, cropped, brown hair and never seemed to smile; and for reasons unbeknownst to Maya, all the other girls in their class seemed to worship her. They would follow Harriet around the playground like she was some sort of cub leader. On a few occasions, Maya tried to add herself onto the end of the group in the hope that they wouldn't notice and would keep her fingers crossed behind her back wishing that they would accept her as a new member. How wrong she was. On one occasion, the group had been walking for not more than thirty seconds when Harriet turned around and announced in a loud voice, "I think we have an intruder amongst us!"

Maya's face, at the time, had gone bright red with embarrassment and she felt as though her feet were frozen, rooted to where she stood, spotlighted. Her eyes started to well, she didn't know what to do whilst they all stared at her and giggled. Her ears began to ring with the sound of the chant, 'intruder, intruder, we've got an intruder.'

Maya turned around and ran as fast as she could back into the school and hid herself away in the toilets. She sat alone in one of the cubicles for quite some time before she was discovered by Emily, a girl from her class who had been trying to get into the bathroom but found the door obstructed from the inside. Once inside, Emily found Maya passed out on the bathroom floor; her school uniform soaked all the way through; and her hair puffed out to twice the size as usual. The bathroom was flooded. Emily screamed for help and shook Maya repeatedly until she woke up. Water seeped out from the door as they left the toilets and went to find help. From that day forward, Maya became known as the girl who flooded the toilets. Some people found it cool, others thought Maya was weird and to Maya's dismay, Harriet continued to ignore her.

So it was shortly after the bathroom incident, that Maya decided she would no longer allow the meanness of others to upset her and instead, she would teach *them* a lesson; starting with Harriet.

Almost half a year had passed, and Maya had been biding her time, waiting for the perfect moment to enact her revenge. She had made some friends of her own in Year 2 and no longer became visibly upset when Harriet's crew would continue to whisper intruder to her when they were lining up for play. It was Friday lunchtime - Harriet and her minions were walking through the hall carrying their trays filled with fish fingers, chips and peas; it was Fish Finger Friday. Harriet was at the front, leading the way as usual and Maya who was sat near to the back of the hall, noticed that Harriet had a cup of water on her tray, next to her lunch.

> 'This is my chance,' she thought and from under the table, with a flick of her hand, she made Harriet's cup tumble onto the floor.

As Harriet stopped in her tracks to bend down and pick it up, Maya then caused the water which was carried by the girl behind Harriet, to jump out of her cup and land with a splash onto Harriet's head. Harriet let out a horrible scream and stood up straight, her hair dripping from her shoulders onto the floor. She then turned to confront the girl behind her. Maya's little trick had caused quite the commotion - people in the hall began to stare, now engrossed in the lunchtime entertainment. The girl apologised profusely and insisted that she had no idea how it had happened.

Amid her outburst of anger, Harriet had not noticed that the spilt water from her cup had started to trickle towards her and had slowly made its way under her shoes. Maya had taken matters one step further. No sooner had Harriet taken a step forward, when she let out a deafening scream as she lost her footing and slipped backwards onto the lunch hall floor. Laughter from the onlookers could be heard reverberating off of the dining hall walls; and this time, it was Harriet's face that went bright red. She sat up feebly and looked worriedly around the room, her shoulders rounded with embarrassment. She then happened to lock eyes with a very poised and relaxed looking Maya, who stared straight back at Harriet and smiled. After that day, Harriet's popularity at school slowly diminished and instead of her usual following of six, her group shrank to just two. Ironically, one of which was the girl who had allegedly spilled water over her head.

> "Maya, are you okay? You look lost in thought."

> "Yes mum, I was just thinking about Harriet Armstrong."

Verity grimaced slightly and ruffled her hair.

> "I'm sure you are going to meet some lovely people here and make some really good friends Maya. We definitely don't want a repeat of the swimming incident, do we?"

Maya crossed her arms and looked straight ahead through the windscreen, where in the distance she could see a group of boys jostling with each other on the field.

> 'Well, if they're nice to me I'll be nice to them,' thought Maya.

Verity would never forget the last time that Maya had decided to get creative with her powers.

Maya had been part of her local swimming club, in West Hampstead, since she was five years old and on a Saturday morning, Verity would take her to synchronised swimming classes. There were eight girls on the team including Maya and they had a wonderful instructor called Janet, who was from France. Janet had always seen the potential in Maya, and had made her the centre swimmer. The centre position was the most important as they were seen as the lead of the group.

Maya got along with nearly all the girls on her team except one, Annabel. Annabel was a small blonde girl from Germany, who was forever telling anyone that cared to listen, that her mother had taken part in the 1960s Olympic synchronised swimming. She also held her head high when she walked and looked sneeringly down her nose at those she felt were beneath her. Maya felt on edge around her, and this feeling had become worse since she had overheard Annabel express openly, on more than one occasion, that she should be centre swimmer and not Maya.

One Saturday, Maya had just finished getting changed when she heard an all too familiar voice. It was Annabel's and she was talking about Maya to one of the other girls.

"Janet only picks her to be centre because she can hold her breath for longer than any of us, that's all it is. She has no proper form."

The second girl giggled.

"Did you see the way she came out of the water on that second turn? No form at all! She was like a baby seal flapping around."

This time, the girl she was talking to let out a nervous laugh. Maya began to feel the blood drain from her face and slowly started to clench her fists.

'I'll show her,' thought Maya.

Maya swung the cubicle door wide open, glared at Annabel and marched straight past her and stormed out through the doors. Annabel's face quickly froze in horror and the other girl hid her face in shame.

A week had passed since the changing room incident - it was the penultimate practice session before the local borough competition and Maya was ready, ready to teach Annabel a lesson she wouldn't soon forget. The parents had also been invited to stay for this training session so that they could have a preview before the finals. As Maya completed her usual warm-up stretches, she noticed Annabel and one of the other girls whispering to each other and instinctively began to feel very uncomfortable. Her skin tingled each time they lifted their heads over in her direction.

Once the girls had warmed up and were in the water, Janet instructed the team to begin the showpiece. Maya was focused. She bided her time and waited until the three girls formed a triangle around her. Once in position, with the wave of her hand, she began to form a current in the water, just slightly below Annabel. As they were meant to spin and emerge from the water, Maya forced the current up so fast and hard that it swept Annabel to the side and knocked her out of sync. Maya giggled to herself as she watched her struggle to get back to position.

> 'It's working,' she thought and grinned as she found that Annabel's face no longer held its usual look of haughtiness and instead, was quite shaken up.

"Annabel! What do you think you are doing?" yelled Janet. "You must hold your position!"

Maya became giddy with the power as she repeatedly conjured up the current and its tornado-like effect and began to relish seeing Annabel be told off for messing around.

"It's not me Janet, it's the water!" spluttered Annabel in between mouthfuls of water.

Seeing Annabel as visibly distressed as she was, wasn't enough for Maya. She wasn't finished with teaching her a lesson and felt that she deserved more payback. Just enough so that she wouldn't forget. As they neared the end of their piece and were all sat under the water, for the last thirty seconds, before they were meant to rise to the top, Maya created a current just above Annabel's head. She knew her actions were dangerous, but she didn't care. Annabel had to learn her lesson.

> "Annabel, Annabel!" called Janet. "This is no time for messing around, where are you?"

The other seven girls had gracefully floated to the top and remained posed in the swan position. Annabel was nowhere to be seen.

> "There she is Janet, look, she can't seem to get to the top!" shouted one of the girls as she pointed over to where Annabel looked to be struggling to rise below the water's surface.

A few of the girls started to cry as they watched Annabel's arms and legs flay wildly against the current above her. Her mother aghast rushed down to the edge of the pool.

> "Can't you do something?" she called out to Janet in desperation.

Janet moved swiftly to the other side of the pool to get the long pole. Annabel was now really fighting against the current to get to the top. but Maya didn't care and decided to make the current even stronger, causing Annabel's face to turn blue as she gasped for air.

> "She's drowning!" screamed her mother.

Maya finally realised that she had gone too far and immediately stopped the current from circulating above Annabel's head. She then rapidly focused her efforts on directing the current below Annabel, so that it forced her up to the surface.

Janet pulled an unconscious Annabel out of the water and Maya suddenly felt an overwhelming sense of dread build inside of her. She looked around the pool to find a sea of distraught and tearful faces. Annabel's mother's face was anguished. She then saw her own mother staring at her, with a look that was filled with disappointment.

Laid limp in her mother's arms, at the side of the pool, Annabel came round a few minutes later. Her skin pale and her body trembling as she shivered and sobbed. Janet called the session to a close and let the parents know that she would call them all later that evening.

"Mum are you okay?" asked Maya this time round.

Verity looked over at Maya. "Yes hun, come on we had better get your bags out of the car."

"What were you thinking about back there?" asked Maya, as they pulled the suitcases along the gravel path towards the main doors.

"Do you remember what I said to you after the swimming incident a few years ago?"

Maya felt her face go slightly red.

"Yes mum," she replied, slightly begrudgingly.

"You said, it doesn't matter how mean people are to me, I am not to take matters into my own hands again like that, because that's not what my powers are for."

Verity stopped and gave Maya a big hug.

"And that's still true to this day Maya. It doesn't matter how difficult things get whilst you are here, you must remember not to use your powers to be unnecessarily cruel."

Maya looked up at her mother and smiled.

"I know mum, I won't."

They continued up the path until they reached the front door.

Maya had a good feeling about Capel Manor and decided that a new beginning wouldn't be so bad after all.

'Besides, what trouble can I really get into at a boarding school,' she thought to herself.

RUN CHRIS RUN – CHRIS' SHOES

"Oh, don't touch that Chris!" shrieked a young woman with long blonde hair.

Chris had begun to pull at the wire rack that held an assortment of magazines and a few from the bottom rung had started to fall out. The woman, Chris' mum, ran over to him quickly from where she was sitting and scooped him up into her arms and took him away before he could cause any more destruction. Chris was a cute baby who was slightly small for his age; had a head of blonde hair like his mother's and electric blue eyes.

His mother, Jane, was a single parent and was struggling to make ends meet. They lived in a one-bedroomed apartment near Latimer Road in West London, which consisted of a kitchen and front room, which were part of the same room. The bedroom just about fitted a cot and single bed; and the shower was known for being unpredictable; it would often run cold, sometimes for days at a time. Chris' mother worked as a clerk, in a local betting shop on the high street. It was minimum wage and she was on a zero-hours contract. To make matters worse, she struggled to find reliable childcare, which meant that she missed out on shifts. Jane was in trouble, she had fallen behind on her rent and was down to her last fifty-pounds until the end of the month. Chris' father was nowhere to be seen - he had fled the minute that he had found out Jane was pregnant.

Two weeks earlier, Jane had seen an advert online:

'Do you have a two-year-old child? Want to make some extra cash? £3500. Then bring your child along to 164 Brent Street, for clinical trials. Children will be given a vaccine for the common cold, duration one month.'

Whilst she filled out the application form, Jane pushed aside any thoughts of uncertainty and convinced herself that everything would be fine. Just the previous year, she herself had taken the flu vaccine and besides feeling slightly groggy for a day or two, she was fine overall. She also felt that it would more than likely build up Chris' immune system. How wrong she was.

His heart raced and pounded in tandem with each footstep, as it hit the ground. He couldn't stop, he had to keep on going. His eyes now full of tears, began to blur his vision of the cars and people that he passed by at light speed. Chris tried to block out the wailing sirens and the murmur of people's voices.

He had to get away from them, he couldn't take it anymore. The pavement was overcrowded with people and each building he passed felt intimidatingly large and cast a looming shadow over him. He was nearly there, almost at his safe space. His mind a frenzy, Chris ignored the red traffic light and darted across the road.

Screeeeech!

Chris looked over his shoulder to find a car awkwardly stopped in the middle of the pedestrian crossing and skid marks imprinted on the road where the driver had come to a halt.

'Almost there,' thought Chris.

He slowed his pace to a walk as he entered the park and made his way to his usual hideout; an undisclosed cabin that sat just behind the wildlife reserve. This was Chris' safe space and had been since he was six years old, when he had gotten into his first fight with another child in the playground.

Chris sat with his knees huddled to his chest and with his head drooped down between them. His bottom rested on the hard wooden floor of the cabin and his back leant against the wall. He began to cry.

"Why does everybody hate me?" he sobbed out loud. "Why me, what's wrong with me?"

Earlier that morning, Jane had received a call from Chris' school. He had been in another fight. A boy from his class had accused him of cheating during a game of football. If there was one thing Chris hated, it was being called a cheat. He also had a tendency to be rather hot-headed.

> "Oh Chris, not again!" exclaimed Jane as she found herself once more sat opposite the head teacher.
>
> "It wasn't my fault mum," snapped Chris from the chair beside her. "It was that idiot Noah!"
>
> "Chris, don't be so rude," retorted Jane.

This was the third time in the last month that Chris had been involved in an altercation with another pupil. The head teacher, Mr Davey, had become quite accustomed to the back-and-forth between Chris and his mother.

> "If I may," he interjected.

It was no use, Chris' mother had had enough.

> "You do know I've had to leave halfway through a shift because of you! Why do you have to be so selfish Chris, why can't you just behave?"

Chris' face went bright red with anger and his

jaw visibly clenched as he gritted his teeth.

> "I hate you!" shouted Chris. "You never take my side, you always blame me."

He stood up sharply causing his chair to fall backwards onto the floor.

> "Okay, let's all calm down," said Mr Davey rather desperately.

It was too late, Chris had decided he wasn't going to stick around for another telling off and took off through the office door, bumping into one of his friends as he ran down the corridor, ignoring him as he shouted after him. Once out of the building and on the streets, he continued run and headed towards his safe space.

Chris awoke to the sound of his name being called by an unfamiliar voice. He had fallen asleep in the cabin and now felt very disorientated. Several hours had passed and it was dark outside. As he peered out from the cabin window, he could faintly make out the wildlife reserve; and somewhere far in the distance, he could see what looked like a glow from the light of a torch.

"Chris, CHRIS! Are you here?" the voice bellowed again.

Chris backed away from the window and sat down once more.

"What's mum done?" he muttered angrily to himself. "Why can't she just leave me alone?"

A few hours earlier, after frantically searching the apartment and knocking on her neighbours doors, Chris' mother, who was wrought with worry, had done what any mother would have in the same situation. She had called the police and declared Chris as missing.

The policeman she spoke to on the phone at the time wasn't the most helpful and kept asking her to describe Chris, insisting that she gave him more details on what he was wearing.

"For goodness sake!" snapped Jane down the phone. "How many times do I have to tell you? He's about five feet two, skinny, bright blonde hair and he has blue eyes! What more do you want from me?"

> "I'm just trying to get a full picture of him madam and I would appreciate it if you would calm down."
>
> "And I'm trying to tell *you* that my son, who is only ten years old, is out there somewhere, alone! Anything could have happened. And if you ask me one more time to describe his school uniform I'll…"

Jane didn't get to finish her sentence and instead jumped at the unexpected sound of a knock at the door.

> "Chris?" she called out as she opened the door.

It wasn't Chris. At the door stood a policewoman and a very tall, unassuming man with brown hair.

> "Ms Allen, are you still there?" came the voice from her phone that was still firmly held to her ear.
>
> "Yes, there's a police officer at my door and some man, did you send them here?" she asked nervously.

> "Oh yes, sorry, I forgot to mention that as part of our missing child protocol, for four to eleven-year-olds, we now send an officer to the family home, along with a child psychologist. They're there to help you remember anything that might be useful."

Chris' mother ended the call, she had had enough of the police officer's incompetence.

> "Please tell me you can help me?" she asked desperately to the two strangers at the door.

Once inside, Jane relayed to them the events that had unfolded earlier that day at school and explained that this wasn't the first time Chris had tried to run away.

The police officer listened and took notes on her pad. The brown-haired gentleman seemed to listen intently and had a look of calm about him that Jane wasn't sure what to make of.

> "When you say he ran away before, where was it?" asked the man.

Jane fidgeted in her chair.

"He was just six years old and we were in Avondale Park, he and another boy had got into a fight over a toy in the sand pit. Chris kicked the boy and so I shouted at him and he ran off. He's just so fast you see, and hard to catch so I couldn't keep up with him but we managed to find him after about twenty minutes…"

Jane stopped talking and buried her head into her hands and sighed.

"I think I know where he is," she said quietly, her face now in a semi-relieved state.

The educational psychologist smiled and looked at the police officer who then spoke into her walkie-talkie.

"Let's go and find Chris," he said.

The once-distant glow from the torches neared and the voices became louder.

"Chris, are you here? Answer me!"

Chris grimaced as he heard his mother's voice this time.

> "There you are!" squealed Jane and ran over to hug him.

> "Go away!" said Chris firmly.

A tear dropped down Jane's face and she took a step back.

> "I'm sorry Chris," she began.

Chris turned his head to face the wall nearest to his right shoulder.

> "Jane, do you mind if I try?" asked the brown-haired man. "He might just need a not-so-familiar face right now."

Jane nodded and wiped her eyes as she made her way out of the cabin.

> "Who are you?" snapped Chris at the stranger.

> "Chris, my name is Dr Andrew Ashworth. I'm an educational psychologist and believe it or not, I have been looking for you for quite some time now."

Chris' eyes narrowed inquisitively as he looked over in the direction of this Dr Ashworth.

"Looking for me, why?" asked Chris.

Dr Ashworth entered the cabin and positioned himself on the floor next to Chris.

"Chris, has your mother ever spoken to you about the doctor's surgery in London Bridge?"

"A doctor's surgery, no why would she?" replied Chris. His face looked puzzled and his eyebrows had gone slightly inwards, as they did when he felt slightly suspicious of something.

"It's quite a long story Chris and I don't think we have enough time for that tonight. However, I want you to know that you are unique Chris and that you and I being here in this cabin is not by chance."

Dr Ashworth brushed his trousers down as he stood up. Looking fondly at Chris, he said "I'm going to ask your mother if I am able to pop round tomorrow so we can finish our conversation. How does that sound?"

Chris nodded.

Once home, Chris confronted his mother about the doctor's surgery that Dr Ashworth had mentioned to him.

Chris' mother avoided all eye contact and he could have sworn that she winced when he said the words London Bridge.

> "What is it mum?" raged Chris. "What are you not telling me?"

Jane broke down in tears and instead of answering Chris' questions she kept apologising.

> "Fine!" shouted Chris, "I'll just find out tomorrow!" and stormed off towards his room.

The sign that hung above his door swayed from left to right and rattled as his door shut with a bang.

The next morning could not have come around

quickly enough for Chris. He sat at the breakfast table, his face just as disgruntled as the night before and glared at his mum whilst he ate his cereal.

> "Dr Ashworth will be here in an hour Chris, he wants to start some therapy sessions with you. Might be good for you."

Chris kept his eyes down and focused on his bowl.

> "Chris are you listening to me?" asked Jane. "I just said the man from last night, Dr Ashworth, is coming to see you. I think he said he'll take you to the park."

Chris shrugged his shoulders nonchalantly.

True to his word, Dr Ashworth arrived promptly at eleven A.M. It was a crisp, bright sunny morning as they walked slowly towards the park making small talk as they went.

> "Why are we here?" asked Chris quite impatiently.

"Good question Chris and I have one for you."

Chris cocked his head upwards to look at Dr Ashworth, he felt rather puzzled.

"Who is the fastest man in the world right now?" asked Dr Ashworth.

"That's easy," said Chris and grinned as he answered, "Usain Bolt".

Dr Ashworth smiled, "I thought you might say that, but you're wrong."

"No way," said Chris. "He is! Last summer he did the 100 metres in 9.58 seconds, there's no one faster than that."

"Actually, there is Chris."

"What?!" exclaimed Chris. "Who?"

Dr Ashworth stopped walking and looked directly at Chris and paused before he answered, "You."

> "Me?" exclaimed Chris. "Yeah right. I know I'm good at football and everything but no one is faster than Usain."
>
> "I think there's only one way to prove it then," said Dr Ashworth and took his phone out from his trouser pocket.
>
> "You see that tree over there, just past the bin. I want you to run all the way there and back as fast as you can. It should be about one hundred metres give or take."

Chris laughed, "Okay," he said.

> "I'll record you," said Dr Ashworth. "This way you can see just how fast you are."
>
> "Ready, steady, GO!" shouted Dr Ashworth.

Chris took off as fast as he could, he felt exhilarated and free as he ran through the park which was pretty much empty apart from a dog walker in the distance. Once back by Dr Ashworth's side, he asked, "how did I do?"

Dr Ashworth grinned and pressed play on his phone.

> "I don't get it," said Chris. "You can see me start to run but then there's nothing there."

> "Look a little closer," said Dr Ashworth.

Chris looked again and this time he could make out a faint blur, moving at an extreme speed in the same direction that he had run and then right back towards where they stood. Chris also noticed that the recording was only four seconds long in total.

> "Is that..?"

> "Yes", interjected Dr Ashworth. "That is indeed you Chris."

The next hour flew by and the more Chris listened to Dr Ashworth explain what had happened to him as a baby and why he had always felt different from other children, he felt as though a great weight had been lifted off his shoulders. It all made sense to him now.

> 'This is why all the other kids always say that I'm cheating somehow,' he thought. 'And no wonder mum kept on saying sorry last night.'

As they ventured back to the apartment, Chris couldn't help but wonder what he was meant to do with his newfound powers.

> "Dr Ashworth, what happens now?" he asked.
>
> "Now Chris, we have work to do and time is of the essence."

NO ONE LIKES BEING LONELY – JAVIER

"We have to try something different Jose, what choice do we have?"

Jose scratched his head and sighed deeply before he spoke.

> "Okay, let's give him a call," he said apprehensively.

Paula, Jose's wife began to dial the number shown on the business card she held in her left hand and looked hopefully at her husband as she held her phone to her right ear.

> "Hello, Dr Ashworth speaking, how can I help you?"

The Mendez family had emigrated from Spain to England when their son Javier was just a year old and had managed to find accommodation in Hornsey, North London. Javier's father, Jose, worked for an uncle in the family-run Tapas restaurant in the heart of Camden. Paula, Javier's mother, worked as a nanny in the local area. This was ideal for her as it meant she could look after Javier at the same time and not have to worry about paying for childcare. Their financial situation saddened Paula as she was a qualified teacher back in Spain and longed to be able to teach in the UK. However, she, like many Europeans, found that her qualifications in Britain didn't really amount to much and to be able to work as a teacher in England, she would have to re-train. This, like being able to afford childcare, was not an option.

Their son Javier, who was now nine years old, had become increasingly quiet and markedly distant at home. He was struggling at school and often found himself isolated and unable to make friends. Javier had always been different and ever since he was four years old, his parents noticed that he had a penchant for staring at the brick walls of buildings; almost as though he was able to see something that no one else could.

"Oh Dr Ashworth, I am so happy you picked up!" exclaimed Paula into the phone.

Jose sat nervously at the kitchen table, warming his hands on his cup of coffee.

"How can I help you?" asked the voice from the other end of the call.

"We really need your help Dr

Ashworth, it's got worse."

Jose stood up to comfort Paula as she began to sob and placed his arms around her sunken shoulders.

"Do you remember when you came to visit Javier at school last year?"

"I do," replied Dr Ashworth, "and I'm glad that you have decided to call."

A year prior, Javier had been in class, sitting on the carpet for story time, when he became distracted with the sounds that stemmed from the classroom next door. His mind drifted off as he started to imagine what the other children were doing in there. Before he knew what was happening, he found himself in the classroom next door. It was like the wall no longer existed between the two rooms and he was now able to see the children from the other class as clearly as he could his own peers. Class 3RC were having a music lesson and were singing along with their teacher who was playing the guitar. Javier, who was really enjoying being able to watch and be part of the lesson, had no idea that he was in fact seeing directly through the wall.

"Aaaaaaaaagh!"

The girl who was sat next to Javier had let out a very loud and shrill scream and within seconds, the wall was there again and he was back in his classroom. As Javier looked around the room, he was confronted with a myriad of scared and horrified faces staring right at him, one of which was his teacher's. Although she tried to hide it, Javier felt her unease every time she looked at him. He tucked his legs up to his chest and hid his head in between his knees. He had no idea what had happened and really didn't understand why his classmates looked so afraid of him. Even though twenty-eight sets of eyes remained fixed on him, he had never felt so alone in his life.

His teacher made her way to the classroom door, beckoned a member of staff from the hallway and instructed them to take Javier to the medical room until the end of the day.

'What have I done?' thought Javier. 'Why am I here?'

Just before home time, his teacher came to see him and hesitantly explained why his friends had looked so afraid. Javier sat in shock whilst he listened to his teacher describe: how his body had stiffened up; how his eyes had widened unnaturally so; and, how they had frozen in position. The classroom incident marked a pivotal moment in Javier's life and he began to use his newfound powers at every opportunity. He now had a secret of his own, something that no one could take from him. Javier soon learnt not to care what the others said about him, no matter how hurtful some of the comments were and he had also accepted that appearing possessed in the middle of the playground, or halfway through an assembly wasn't going to win him any friends; and he had even grown used to some of the older kids calling him names each time they saw him.

> "Look there's Zombie Boy," they would call out as they walked past him in the playground. And - "How's Mental Martian doing today?" they asked him in the hallway.

Javier's episodes had become so bad that his teacher suggested to his parents that they apply to have an educational psychologist assess him.

> "When you say it's got worse, what do you mean?" asked Dr Ashworth.

Paula looked at Jose uncertainly and took a deep breath before answering.

> "Something happened the other night," she continued "and now Javier won't come out of his room. He doesn't want to talk to us."
>
> "I see," replied Dr Ashworth.
>
> "He said he's sick of being different, he said he feels cursed."

Paula broke down into tears once more.

> "Paula, are you able to ask Javier to speak with me on the phone? I think it might be easier that way."

As she made her way to Javier's bedroom, Paula thought back to the first educational psychologist that came to see Javier and how, despite her enthusiasm to help, she had no idea what was going on. At the time, the psychologist had diagnosed Javier with having Absence Seizures; and had described it as a condition where the person is both consciously there and at the same time subconsciously not.

> "Javier, it's Dr Ashworth on the phone, he wants to talk to you about what happened the other night."

Paula knocked again. This time Javier opened the door slightly and stretched out his arm for his mum's phone.

> "Hello Dr Ashworth," said Javier wearily.

> "Hello Javier, I hear you have had a bit of a rough time over the last week. Do you want to tell me what happened?"

> "I, I… " began Javier and fell silent once more.

> "It's okay, take your time Javier. Try to describe to me everything that you remember happening."

Javier started again, "I saw a robbery taking place in a shop. I was with my mum and dad and we were walking back from the restaurant at night. It was dark and I knew my parents wouldn't be able to see what I was doing, so I decided to have a look around, you know, use my powers."

"I see," said Dr Ashworth.

"I really wished that I hadn't, Dr Ashworth, because what I saw was horrible."

"What did you see Javier?"

"I had been looking into a newsagent on the other side of the road, which was about fifty metres ahead of us, when I saw a man in a mask who had one of his hands around the shopkeeper's neck."

Dr Ashworth could hear Javier's voice begin to quiver as he continued.

"He also had a gun pointed to her head," stammered Javier. "He was demanding that she take money out of the till and place it into a black bag on the counter. There was also another robber in the shop who was stood by the door, keeping watch."

"That must have been terrifying to witness. What happened next?" asked

Dr Ashworth.

"I could see the fear on the woman's face and I had to watch the tears fall from her eyes as she begged for her life. I decided not to watch anymore and quickly told my mum and dad what was happening."

"And what did they say Javier?"

Javier huffed before answering.

"They didn't believe me of course, why would they? In their eyes, I'm just a kid who was making up stuff."

"In all fairness to them Javier, you must be able to see why they might find it hard to believe that you would know that something quite so eventful was happening from so far away."

"Yeah, they just laughed at me and told me to stop being silly. So I kept on telling them until my dad got really cross and warned me that I would be sent straight to my room when we got back home if I didn't stop with the stories."

"Javier are you okay?" asked Paula from outside the bedroom door.

"Yes mum, I'm fine, I'll come out when I have finished."

"The next day, my mum had gone out to the shops and my dad came to see me in my room. He looked like he had seen a ghost or something and he had a newspaper in his hands. 'Mijo, you were right,' he said and showed me the newspaper." The front page read,

"Local shop owner held at gunpoint."

"He asked me how I knew, so I attempted to explain everything to him."

"So you told him?" asked Dr Ashworth.

"Yes," replied Javier. "He couldn't quite get his head around it at first, so I said that he should go into the living room, while I stayed in the bedroom and asked him to do some things in there. You know, like open drawers or something. When he returned, I described to him exactly what he had done. He couldn't believe it. I think it was the first time that I've seen my father cry. He explained that he was relieved as he thought that maybe I was ill or something but he also begged me not to tell my mum as she would only worry."

Javier took a breath.

"Ever since that day, it has been a secret between me and my father."

"I'm glad that you told him Javier. Keeping secrets is never easy."

"I remember when we first met, do you?" asked Dr Ashworth.

"Yes," replied Javier. "You were with that other educational psychologist, that woman."

Dr Ashworth chuckled.

> "Quite right Javier and it's a good job I was there to sign off on her final observations. The point I'm trying to make is that I knew you were special from the moment we met and I knew that you would continue to have a hard time fitting in, in a school like that."

> "I hate it there," said Javier quickly.

> "I know Javier, but there's little we can do about that for now. However, I do have an idea."

Javier's ears pricked up and he sat straighter in his chair.

> "What idea?" he asked eagerly.

> "I'm going to suggest to your parents that at the end of Year 6 you come to Capel Manor Boarding School to continue your education. This way I can continue to help you learn to harness your powers."

Javier's face beamed with excitement and he couldn't stop himself from shouting *YES!*

whilst he punched the air.

> "Very good," said Dr Ashworth. "Although I have the feeling it is going to take your mum a bit more convincing."

Two weeks later, as promised, Dr Ashworth went to visit the Mendez family at their flat in Hornsey.

Crammed together around the small kitchen table, they spoke at great length about Capel Manor Boarding School and leafed through the school prospectus. As predicted, Javier's mother, Paula, was immediately opposed to the idea.

> "No Jose, he's not going. This isn't open for discussion, he's just a little boy!"

Before his father was able to answer, Javier interrupted. "I'm not so little anymore mum, I can take care of myself."

Paula laughed.

> "Javier, you are my only child, I won't let you go, you can stay here in London and go to Camden High as we planned."

> "But mum, these kids are nothing like me. I don't want to go to Camden High, they won't understand me."

Javier's eyes darted desperately from Dr Ashworth to his father and back to Dr Ashworth in the hope of some support. Javier's dad closed his eyes and sighed.

> "Now might be a good time Javier," said Dr Ashworth cautiously.

> "A good time for what?" asked Paula. "What's going on, Jose why do you have that look on your face?"

Javier looked at his father once more and this time felt a weight lifted from him as his father nodded and smiled warmly at him.

Paula listened as Javier spoke for the next five minutes and she listened some more as he described what he had worked out he was able to do with his eyes since he was just six years old. She sat quietly and didn't utter a word whilst he spoke about what he and Dr Ashworth had been practicing in their sessions. And she was even silent whilst Javier re-told the story of the night of the burglary and how he had shown his father his powers.

> "Mum are you okay?" asked Javier, once he had finished.

Paula burst into tears and squeezed him tight.

> "I always knew there was something special about you mijo. I just felt it all these years."

> "You're not upset at me for not telling you?" asked Javier.

> "No, how could I be, besides it is kind of my fault after all."

Javier looked puzzled.

> "If I may, Paula?" interjected Dr Ashworth.

Paula nodded her head and continued to wipe away any remaining tears.

> "Javier, your mother is referring to the

clinical trials that you were part of as a baby. We have spoken about this briefly before."

"Oh yeah," said Javier. "You said that there were five of us all together at the trial and we were all injected with some sort of test sample."

Jose grimaced as he heard the words test sample.

"Yes, and from the information I have managed to acquire over the years, that was never the intention, well at least not from the lead clinician who was carrying out the trial."

"I'm so sorry," burst out Paula. "I'm sorry you have to live like this mijo."

"It's okay mum, it's quite cool really, I like being able to do something that no one else can do. It makes me feel special."

Paula smiled weakly at Javier.

"The most important thing is that I managed to find you Javier, and in good time too." Continued Dr Ashworth. "I have also found the others, well, all apart from one."

"Really?" exclaimed Javier in amazement.

"Yes really," replied Dr Ashworth with a smile. "They will also be attending Capel Manor next September, so you will have plenty of time to get to know them."

A warm fluttery feeling came over Javier.

"Please mum can I go, please? I don't want to be alone anymore. It's lonely being me."

Paula looked at Jose who looked back at her and nodded in approval.

"Yes mijo, you can go."

Javier almost threw himself across the table to hug his parents.

"Thank you!" he exclaimed excitedly, as they both hugged their little boy tight.

HIDE AND SEEK - AMY'S WORLD

Amy and her mother lived together in Fulham, South West London. They had a small house that was part of a mews and was just a short walk from the ever-frequented Kings Road. It had been just the two of them since Amy could remember - tragically, Amy's father had died from a stroke just months after she was born. Amy's mother, Alison, was left distraught, her whole world had crumbled around her. All the plans she and her husband had made were now non-existent. The promise of a happy future, the imagined car trips as a threesome, now faded. To say that the year of her husband's death had been exceptionally hard for Alison would be an understatement; as each day passed, she felt more and more hopeless and wondered how she would manage to raise their child on her own. Fortunately, Alison's husband had taken out a life insurance policy the year before Amy was born, which meant that Alison was able to put a large deposit down on the two-bedroom house in Fulham.

Both Amy and her mother were blonde-haired and had emerald-green eyes, and when stood next to each other, even at Amy's very young age, they looked strikingly alike. Three years had passed since the death of her husband and Alison had adapted to her new life with Amy.

It had gone dark outside and Alison had just finished laying Amy down in her cot and was about to sit down to read her a story, when she realised that she had left Amy's book in the living room, so went downstairs to get it. On her return, Alison shrieked.

"Amy! where are you?" she called out in a panic.

Amy was nowhere to be seen, she wasn't in her cot and Alison couldn't see her anywhere in the bedroom. Amy had never climbed out of her cot before and it was such a high cot that if she had managed to climb out she would have heard her fall. Alison's mind began to race with worst-case scenarios as she looked frantically around the room. She wasn't under the rocking chair and she wasn't in the wardrobe.

> 'Where is she?' thought Alison as she pulled at her hair. 'What if someone has snatched her, what if someone is in the house?'

She stood in the middle of the room and clutched her head in despair and with the back of her hand she wiped away the tears. Then, suddenly, as if someone had answered her prayers, there lay Amy in her cot. Alison wept in disbelief as Amy looked up at her with her big green eyes and smiled.

> 'I must be going mad,' she thought as she swept Amy out of her cot and held

her tight.

"What's wrong with me," she muttered out loud. "You're freaking out Alison, Amy was here the whole time. Get a grip!"

"I think you'll be happy here," said Alison. "Do you like your room?"

Amy shrugged and continued to hang up some of her clothes in the wardrobe.

"I wonder who your room-mate will be?" Alison continued.

"I don't care," replied Amy flippantly. "They probably won't like me anyway."

"Oh don't say that Amy, you just take a while to warm up to people, that's all."

Amy was now ten years old and not quite so little anymore, although she still had the same rounded face, long blonde hair and big green eyes. They had not long arrived at Capel Manor Boarding School and had begun to unpack.

Amy sat on her bed and began to fiddle with the keychain on her rucksack. Her mum was right, she did take a while to warm up to others and if she had it her way, she would rather not have to socialise with people her own age.

> "Just promise me that you won't do any of your *disappearing* acts Amy."

Amy looked at her mother and smirked.

> "I mean it Amy, you really mustn't draw attention to yourself whilst you are here. This is a fresh start for you."

> "How will I draw attention to myself if no one even knows where I am?" replied Amy facetiously.

Alison ruffled her hair and went to sit next to Amy on the bed. "You know what I mean Amy, don't be smart."

> "Okay mum," sighed Amy. "I'll be on my best behaviour and I'll try to make friends."

Alison didn't look so convinced.

"I'm going to have to go now Amy, it's getting late."

Amy looked at the time on her phone, 18.38.

"Okay mum," she replied.

"I'll be back in just two weekends, we can go somewhere nice to eat in town. How does that sound?"

Amy nodded and forced a smile.

"I'll miss you poppet, be good!" said Alison, as she gave Amy one last hug and headed towards the door.

Once alone in her new dwellings, Amy threw herself onto her bed and began to cry. She felt alone again and did not want to be by herself in this strange school. She also felt apprehensive with thoughts of her roommate who was due to arrive the next day and began to worry about what she might be like.

Amy decided she needed to do something to take her mind off things. She sat up and reached into her rucksack at the end of the bed and pulled out her diary; an extremely thick bound notepad that she had used to journal her thoughts over the past three years. The diary was her mother's idea as Amy wasn't one for words and especially didn't like talking about her feelings; *especially* not with her mother. Over time, they had agreed that Amy would let her mum read her diary entries once every two weeks.

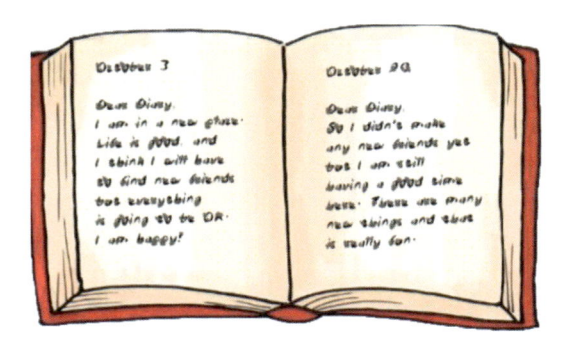

As Amy flicked towards the back of her diary, to write down how she was feeling, the words January 2015 - Hide and Seek caught her eye. She lay back onto her pillow and decided to revisit that event.

Dear Diary,

Today was the worst day of my life, the girls in my class are just so mean, why do they have to be like this? They just don't understand me and I definitely don't understand them, we're just so different. They don't want to get to know me and I certainly don't want to get to know them. We're just from completely different worlds. They think they're so perfect and always go on about their perfect little lives and they always are horrible to me about not having a dad. It's not my fault that my dad is not alive, why do they always have to rub it in my face?

It was just after break and we were lining up to go back into class when I heard them whispering about me and sniggering as usual at the back of the line. I couldn't take it anymore and I decided to confront them. I turned around and marched right up to them. Georgina, Stacey-Ann and Charlotte all went quiet as I faced them. "I hate you!" I shouted at them, "I hate you all!" Mrs Reynolds who had just opened the classroom door heard everything and called me over. "You're in trouble," I heard Georgina say in her annoying voice. It made me so mad that I just left the line and ran down the corridor and I didn't look back. I thought well they don't want me around so I won't be around anymore. I heard Mrs Reynolds calling after me but I didn't care. As soon as I got round the corner I turned myself invisible. I didn't want anyone to find me. I walked around the school for a long time, it felt good knowing that people couldn't see me. I did feel a little bit bad seeing the site manager and the head teacher go past me at least three times with their walkie-talkies. But I just didn't want to be found, not yet anyway. I started to get bored after a while and decided that maybe I should go back to class. As I turned the corner, I saw them all. Mrs Reynolds was taking them for Friday afternoon assembly. They hadn't noticed me because I was still invisible, I had forgotten to turn myself back. Then an idea popped into my head.

I thought that those mean girls deserved a fright. So I joined the back of the line and followed everyone into assembly. The hall was already filling up with the other classes, so I didn't have to worry too much about banging into anyone. I saw that my teacher still had a worried look on her face as she told everyone to sit down, this made me feel sad. I knew I had to be careful at this point and crept along the row stealthily. Still, no one could see me and I sat down in the empty row in front of Stacey-Ann. I was sat in the space where the teachers usually patrol to catch anyone talking. After about ten minutes, I decided that it was time and I turned around to face them. I made myself visible and shouted Boo! right in their faces. You should have heard them scream. Charlotte's face went a bright white, Stacy-Ann looked terrified as she clutched onto Georgina and Georgina burst into tears. Miss Reynolds came rushing over and asked what on earth was going on and then she saw me. She also looked very confused. She also looked relieved at the same time. Mrs Reynold waved her hand over to the head teacher who came rushing over and they took me out of assembly. Once we were outside the hall, they asked me where I had been and if I was okay. The headteacher then took me to the front office where my mum was waiting with her not so impressed face.

Amy stopped reading for a moment and closed her eyes as she thought back fondly on the memory. She decided to re-read a few more of her past entries before she detailed how she was currently feeling and flicked through some more pages until she reached, May 2017 London Zoo.

A smile began to form on Amy's face as she

cast her eyes over the first line.

'Dear Diary,

They deserved it!'

Amy awoke the next morning to a knock on her bedroom door.

"Hi, I'm Sarah," said the rather tall and sporty-looking stranger at the door.

"Hi," replied Amy.

"I'm your new room-mate, are you going to let me in?" she asked. "My parents are downstairs, you might want to get dressed as well," she giggled.

Amy didn't know what to make of Sarah and decided that she had best let her in and figure her out later. She hurried over towards her bed, grabbed her clothes and quickly closed her diary from where it had been left open the night before. She then made her way to the bathroom to get changed. Once dressed, Amy opened the bathroom door to be greeted by a conveyor belt of luggage which passed from who she assumed was Sarah's older brother, to her dad, to her mum and then finally onto the floor in the middle of the room. She sidestepped the incoming luggage and darted towards the door, hoping not to be seen.

"Is this your room-mate Sarah?" asked the older boy.

Amy wasn't quick enough.

"Yes, that's Amy," she replied.

"Hello," said Amy as she stood awkwardly in the doorway before turning swiftly to make her way down to the hall for breakfast.

Later, on the way back to her room she cast her mind back to Sarah and decided it was too soon to make up her mind about her and felt that maybe she should give her a chance. Besides, Amy remembered that she had told her mum that she would try to make friends.

The blood drained from Amy's face as she opened the bedroom door to find Sarah lying on her bed, reading her diary. Any thoughts of making friends with Sarah quickly vanished.

"What do you think you are doing?" yelled Amy.

Sarah jumped and immediately dropped the diary.

"That's private! You have no right!"

"I'm sorry," stuttered Sarah. "It was just lying there, I couldn't help it."

"Yes you could have," said Amy, as she marched towards her and snatched her diary from the bed. "Everyone knows not to go through other people's things. And get off my bed!"

Sarah's cheeks had gone a bright red; she hopped off the bed and headed quickly towards her side of the room.

"Amy, I really am sorry," said Sarah once more. "But can I ask you a question?"

"What?" snapped Amy.

"In some of your stories, you write that you are able to disappear, what's all that about?"

Amy's face now went crimson red and she turned to face Sarah.

"Are you some kind of fantasy novel writer or something?"

Amy exhaled and nodded, the hot red feeling in her cheeks slowly started to dissipate.

"I really like it," said Sarah. "It's kinda cool."

Amy's fists gradually began to unclench.

"Thank you," Amy replied. "But you mustn't tell anyone about my diary, it's private. Okay?"

"I promise," said Sarah whilst she nodded.

Later that evening, when the lights went out, Amy lay in bed and thought,

'Maybe it won't be so bad here after all, at least I have made one friend already.'

ABOUT THE AUTHOR

Kai Harper is the author of the Five Worlds Apart Series and has a background in both the film industry as a production designer and in education as a primary school teacher. Kai grew up in North London and uses his unique experiences in multicultural communities and knowledge of differing social demographics to shape his writing. He has a passion for creating characters in his books that resemble the cohort of friends and acquaintances that he had and met growing up in inner-city London. Kai feels it is important for more mainstream books to have an ever-growing representation of what friendship and adventure can look like amongst an ethnically diverse and urban group of young people. Creating relatable role models for young people is at the heart of his writing.

Having grown up with parents and grandparents who were teachers, deputy heads and head teachers Kai grew up surrounded by books and developed an interest in writing early on, which was further inspired by an author who visited his primary school in Haringey.

Keep an eye out for Five Worlds Apart - Together Again

Luke and his friends have been assigned the task of taking down Robert Mann, Robotics and Artificial Intelligence extraordinaire. As they make their way through a number of dangerous missions, they must also navigate and manage their feelings and friendships all whilst attending school during the day. The clock is ticking and they must prevent Robert Mann and his promise of a brighter future, for civilisation, from destroying the world as they know it.

Follow Author K Harper to keep up with his latest publications

www.kharperwriting.com

#kharperwrites